Usborne
Build your own
TRAINS
Sticker Book

Illustrated by Adrian Mann

Designed by Marc Maynard
Written by Simon Tudhope

Consultant: Andy Coates

Contents

Steam train

This train sounded like a mighty animal panting down the tracks. Powered by the huge boiler in front of the driver, it used high-pressure steam to drive its wheels.

STATISTICS

Active: 1924 – 1964

Top speed: 65mph (105km/h)

Length: 22m

Weight: 70 tonnes

Horsepower: 1,600hp

High speed train

One of the fastest trains on the planet. Fields and trees flash past as it surges between major cities at over 200mph.

STATISTICS

Active: 2012 – present

Top speed: 224mph (360km/h)

Length: 22.8m

Weight: 40 tonnes

Horsepower: 16,300hp

Shunting locomotive

This stocky machine shunts wagons around railway yards. Built for huge power at low speeds, it can handle freight twenty times its own weight.

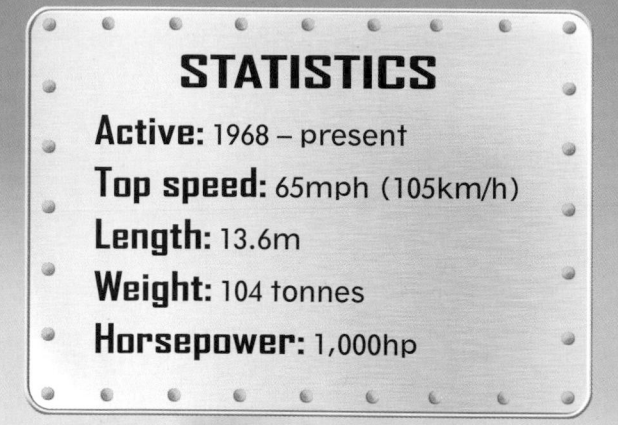

Electric train

Running on busy routes between towns and cities, this train draws all its power from overhead lines. It's fast, quiet and completely smoke-free.

STATISTICS

Active: 2010 – present
Top speed: 100mph (160km/h)
Length: 23m
Weight: 45 tonnes
Horsepower: 2,100hp

Cog locomotive

With its cog wheels gripping the track, this curious machine climbs steep mountain slopes. As it huffs and puffs towards the summit, the boiler's kept flat so it won't overheat.

STATISTICS

Active: 1908 – present

Top speed: 5mph (7km/h)

Length: 5m

Weight: 12 tonnes

Horsepower: 600hp

Tram

This vehicle glides around town along tracks in the road. Drawing its power from overhead lines, it's the smoothest way to travel through the busy streets.

102

Freight train

Clattering across the lonely plains, wheels screeching as it rounds the bends, this train is over one hundred wagons long and packed with heavy freight.

STATISTICS

Active: 1972 – present

Top speed: 65mph (105km/h)

Length: 18m

Weight: 113 tonnes

Horsepower: 4,000hp

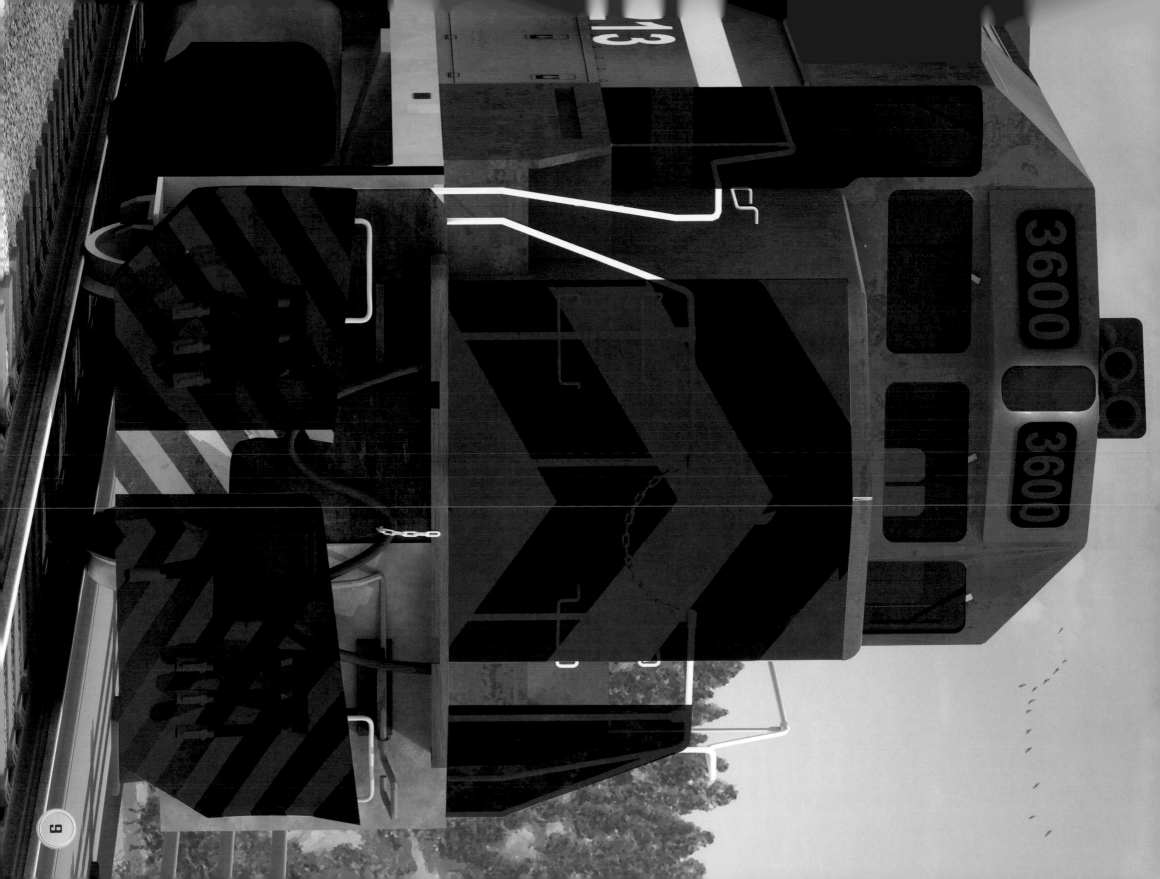

STATISTICS

Active: 2001 – present
Top speed: 22mph (36km/h)
Length: 10.5m
Weight: 15 tonnes
Horsepower: 680hp

Funicular

These little carriages run on separate tracks but work together to climb steep mountain slopes. They're connected by a steel cable, and as one carriage moves down the slope, it pulls the other carriage up.

80

80

Monorail

This train glides around the city on a single rail. The passengers sit back and enjoy the view as it cruises above the busy streets.

STATISTICS

Active: 1988 – present

Top speed: 20mph (33km/h)

Length: 5.6m

Weight: 3.5 tonnes

Horsepower: 300hp

Diesel-electric train

Using a huge diesel engine to generate its own electricity, this train can run anywhere from bustling cities to sleepy country lines.

STATISTICS

Active: 1975 – present
Top speed: 148mph (238km/h)
Length: 17.8m
Weight: 70 tonnes
Horsepower: 2,250hp

43058

Underground train

Here's the train that keeps big cities on the move. Clattering through a network of dark tunnels and brightly-lit stations, it carries thousands of people to work each day.

STATISTICS

Active: 2010 – present

Top speed: 62mph (100km/h)

Length: 17.4m

Weight: 34 tonnes

Horsepower: 3,400hp

Rocket

This is where train travel really began. *Rocket* won a competition to run the world's first steam passenger service. With its engine generating the same power as twenty horses, it blasted transportation into the modern age.

STATISTICS

Active: 1830 – 1840
Top speed: 30mph (48km/h)
Length: 3.7m
Weight: 4.3 tonnes
Horsepower: 20hp

Mallard

The fastest steam locomotive ever built.
With its enormous wheels spinning around
almost nine times every second, *Mallard*
pushed steam power to its limits.

STATISTICS

Active: 1938 – 1963

Top speed: 126mph (203km/h)

Length: 21.3m

Weight: 104.6 tonnes

Horsepower: 1,800hp

Orient Express

It's 1933 and this luxury train is steaming across Europe, from Paris to Istanbul. In the evening, the seats in its oak-panelled compartments are turned into beds, and the restaurant serves fine food and champagne.

EUROPEENS
EXPRESS
GRANDS
ET DES
WAGONS-LITS

SLEEPING CAR

ESSIEUX D'UN BOGIE 2M500

No 3

D'AXE EN AXE DES ESSIEUX EX

STATISTICS

Active: 1915 – 1970

Top speed: 65mph (105km/h)

Length: 16.7m

Weight: 98 tonnes

Horsepower: 1,400hp

Trans-Siberian

Rumbling through 9,000 miles of Russian wilderness, this train is making its way from Moscow to Vladivostok. It takes six days to reach its destination and runs on the longest railway line in the world.

STATISTICS

Active: 1965 – present

Top speed: 62mph (100km/h)

Length: 17.6m

Weight: 117 tonnes

Horsepower: 3,948hp

Channel Tunnel

This high speed train glides under the sea, through a tunnel that connects England to France. You can board in London at 10am and be in Paris in time for lunch.

STATISTICS

Active: 1994 – present
Top speed: 186mph (300km/h)
Length: 22.2m
Weight: 68.5 tonnes
Horsepower: 16,400hp

Flying Scotsman

Charging across the rolling fields, over the hills and bridges, this train ran 400 miles from London to Edinburgh without stopping once on the way.

THE FLYING SCOTSMAN

No. 4472

STATISTICS

Active: 1928 – 1936
Top speed: 100mph (160km/h)
Length: 21.3m
Weight: 98 tonnes
Horsepower: 1,400hp

The Ghan

Running right through the heart of Australia, past snapping crocodiles and scorching deserts, this train travels from Darwin on the north coast to Adelaide on the south.

STATISTICS

Active: 1996 – present
Top speed: 71mph (115km/h)
Length: 22m
Weight: 132 tonnes
Horsepower: 4,020hp

Darjeeling Himalayan Railway

This tough little engine climbs through the foothills of the Himalayas. Nicknamed the 'toy train', it enters each mountain village with a proud toot of its whistle.

STATISTICS

Active: 1889 – present

Top speed: 20mph (32km/h)

Length: 3.7m

Weight: 14 tonnes

Horsepower: 235hp

Glossary

- **BOILER:** a big barrel on a steam locomotive that's in front of the cab. It contains water and steam at high pressure.

- **CAB:** a compartment in a locomotive where the driver works

- **DIESEL ENGINE:** an engine that uses a type of fuel called diesel to generate its power

- **ELECTRIC ENGINE:** an engine that uses electricity to generate its power

- **FREIGHT:** cargo that's transported in large quantities

- **HORSEPOWER:** the power an engine can produce per second. The number in the statistics box is the maximum power that engine can produce.

- **LOCOMOTIVE:** the vehicle on a train that provides the power. This is where the driver works, and is usually at the front of the train.

- **OVERHEAD LINES:** wires above a railway track that carry electricity

- **STREAMLINED:** an object that has been shaped to move through the air as quickly as possible

- **TRAIN:** a locomotive with carriages or wagons attached

Note on the statistics boxes: The 'Length' and 'Weight' measurements are for the front vehicle of each train.

Digital manipulation by Keith Furnival

Edited by Sam Taplin and Phil Clarke

Steam train page 2

High speed train page 3

First Class

380 115

380 115

120

120

120

1002-00213

OLD BETSY

Cog MOUNTAIN Railway

2

102

WESTON PIER

102

MAIN STREET TRAM CO.

WESTON PIER

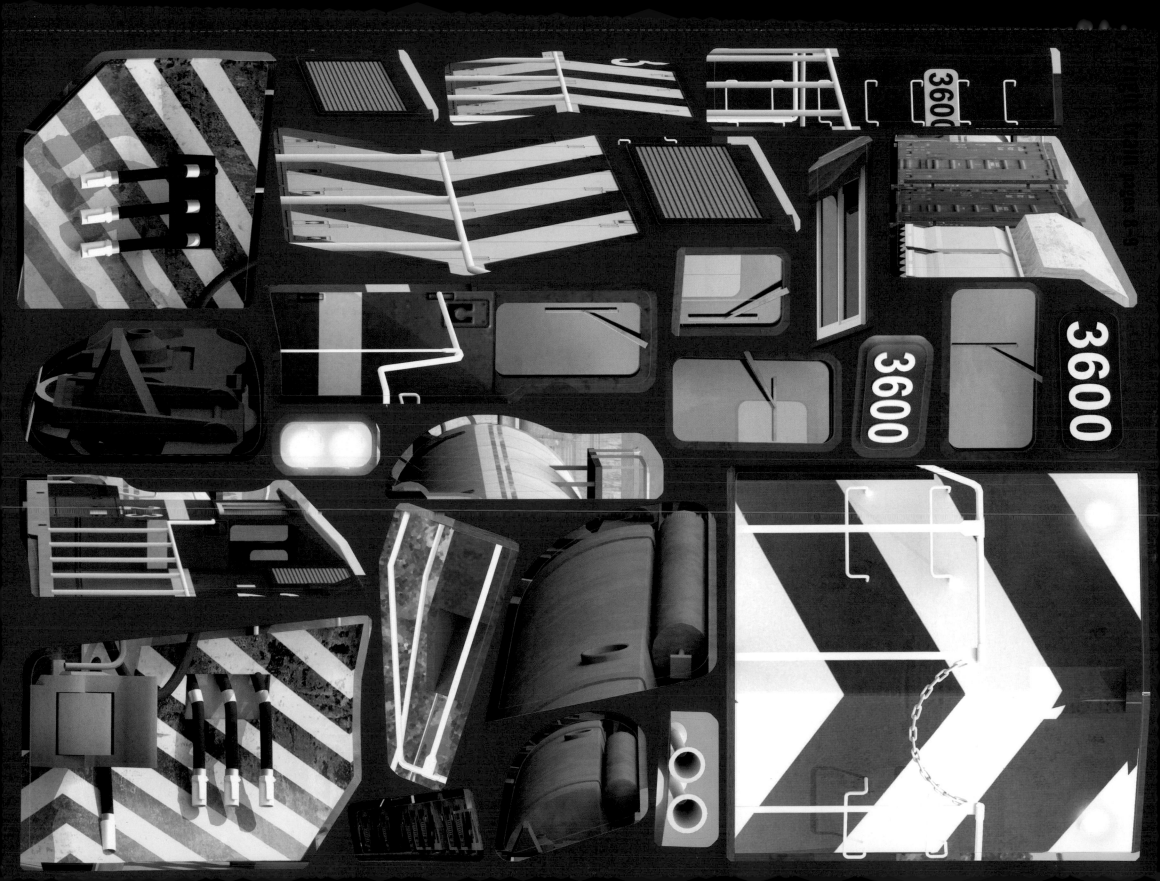

Funicular page 10

Monorail page 11

Diesel-electric train page 12

Connecting the city

80

43058

LIVERPOOL & MANCHESTER RAILWAY — COMPANY

ROCKET

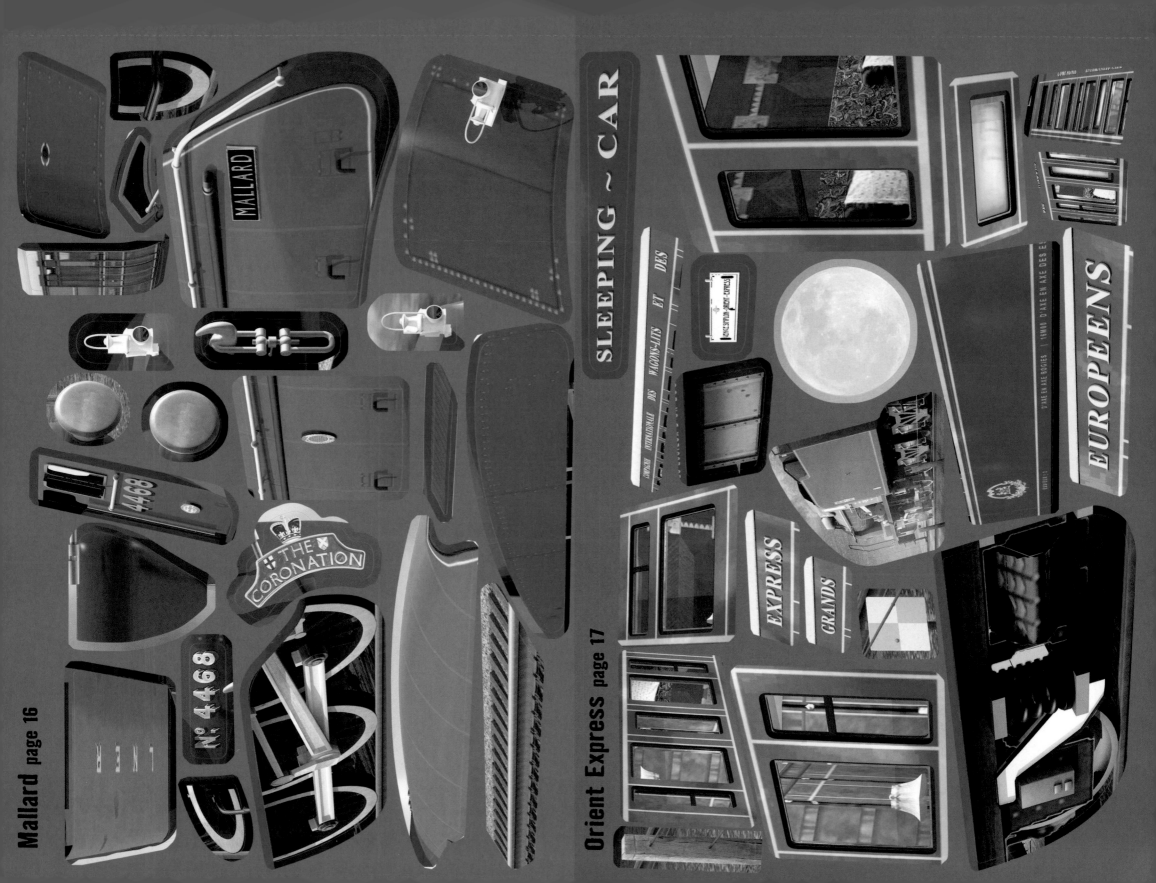

Mallard **page 16**

MALLARD

Nº 4468

4468

Nº 4468

LNER

THE CORONATION

Orient Express **page 17**

SLEEPING ~ CAR

COMPAGNIE INTERNATIONALE DES WAGONS-LITS ET DES

EUROPEENS

EXPRESS

GRANDS

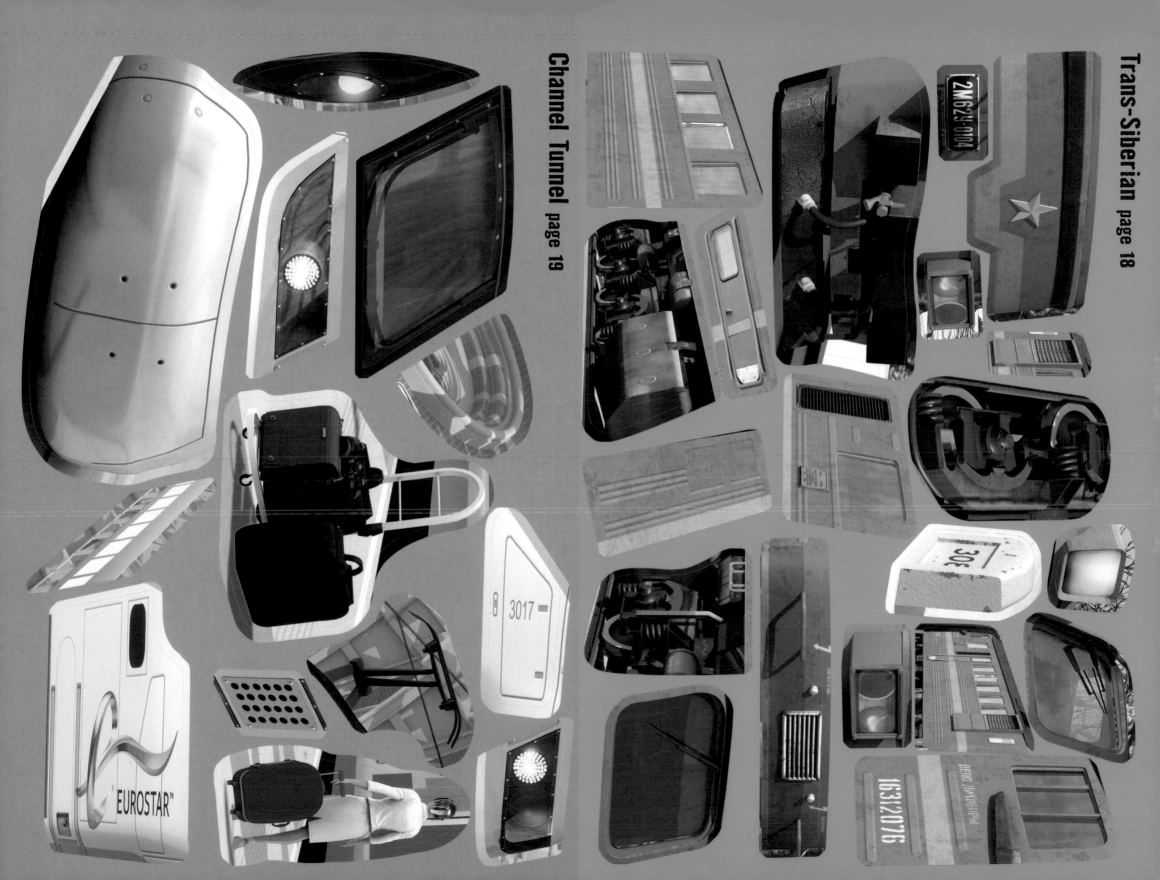

Darjeeling Himalayan Railway page 23

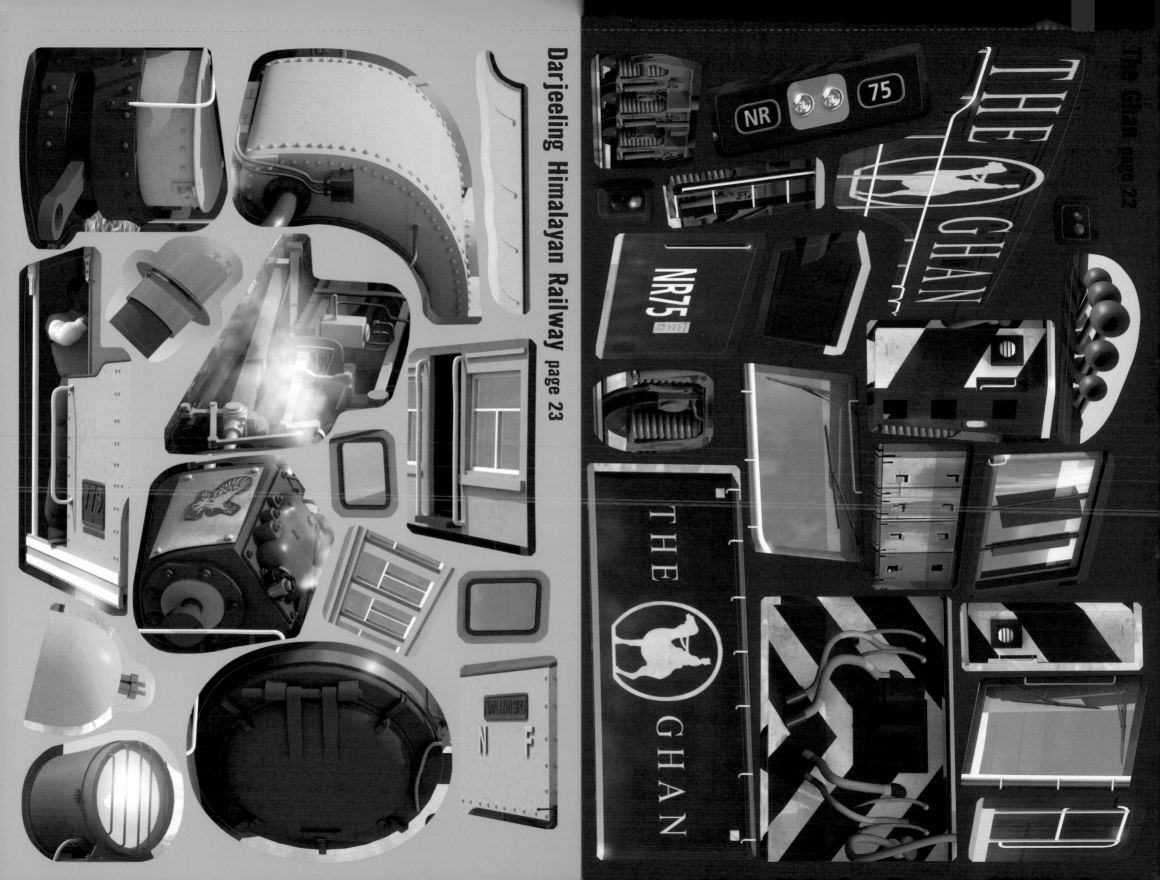

National Railway Museum

Usborne
Build your own
TRAINS
Sticker Book

THE FLYING SCOTSMAN

E R 4472

Nº 4472